ALSO by KEVIN HANSEN

Handersen Publishing, LLC
Lincoln, Nebraska

Junkyard Adventure #8
Weather Witch

Library of Congress Cataloging-in-Publication Data

Names: Hansen, Tevin, author.
Title: Weather witch / Tevin Hansen.
Description: Lincoln, Nebraska : Handersen Publishing, LLC, 2022]
   | Series: Junkyard adventures 8 | Audience: Ages 6-9. | Audience:
   Grades 2-3. | Summary: Siblings Eli and Grace learn about storms
   from Misty the weather witch as they collect emergency supplies
   for a survival kit, rescue a cat from a flooded street, find a magic
   umbrella, and ride magic scooters.
Identifiers: LCCN 2021058623 (print) | LCCN 2021058624 (ebook)
   | ISBN 9781647030599 (paperback) | ISBN 9781647030605
   (hardback) | ISBN 9781647030612 (ebook)
Subjects: CYAC: Weather--Fiction. | Witches--Fiction. | Magic-
   Fiction. | Brothers and sisters--Fiction. | LCGFT: Novels
Classification: LCC PZ7.1.H36433 We 2022 (print) | LCC
   PZ7.1.H36433 (ebook) | DDC [Fic]--dc23
LC record available at https://lccn.loc.gov/2021058623
LC ebook record available at https://lccn.loc.gov/2021058624

Publisher Website: www.HandersenPublishing.com
Publisher Email: editors@HandersenPublishing.com
Author Website: www.TevinHansen.com
Artist Website: loweart.portfoliobox.net

A JUNKYARD ADVENTURE

Tevin Hansen

Handersen Publishing, LLC
Lincoln, Nebraska

Meet Uncle Larry

The junk store on Broadway Street had a million things for sale. And the man who owned the shop had a million stories to tell.

His name was Uncle Larry.

The sign out front…

Uncle Larry's
Antique Shop

…wasn't a complete lie.

There really were antiques inside his store. There were old lamps, paintings with fancy wood frames, art sculptures, baseball and hockey cards, jewelry and furniture, old collectible toys, and lots of other things.

The junkyard was out back.

Uncle Larry had a bunch of junky old cars and trucks that would cost so much to fix that it was cheaper to buy a new one.

Uncle Larry's store also had some of the coolest stuff on the planet. Decades worth of junk and antiques were packed, racked, and stacked into his crowded old shop on Broadway. His apartment was just above the store.

Uncle Larry was a friendly old man who loved to sell things and talk to people. He never married, and never had any children, but he loved to tell stories to kids while their parents shopped in his store.

If it was okay with their moms or dads, or whoever the kids were out shopping with, Uncle Larry would grab his old brown leather stool, plunk right down in the middle of the store, and tell a story.

Uncle Larry had a million stories to tell.

And they always came true.

1
Weather Report

Rainy weather was always a great reason to stay inside and read a good book. Which was exactly what Eli and Grace were doing on such a gloomy afternoon.

Outside, the sky was gray. And the usually busy streets were empty. Neither of them could remember seeing this much rain in such a short amount of time. Even the people on the TV weather station said the city was experiencing record rainfall.

From the living room, Eli and Grace could hear the news report coming from their dad's computer in the downstairs office.

"And now, a look at the weather," announced the meteorologist. "Thunderstorms are expected later this afternoon—including hail. Heavy winds are already coming in from the north. A severe weather alert begins at six o'clock tonight…"

Dad came into the living room holding his empty coffee cup. "You two look nice and cozy on the couch. What are you up to?"

"Reading," said Eli.

"Reading over Eli's shoulder," said Grace. "It's way more fun than reading my own book."

Eli rolled his eyes. "If I read too fast," he explained, "Grace makes me wait until *she's* done reading before I'm allowed to flip the page."

Dad poured himself another cup of coffee. "I was just listening to the news channel," he said from the kitchen. "There's a severe weather warning for later this afternoon. Lots of wind, thunder, lightning, and maybe even some hail."

"Yeah, we know, Dad," said Eli.

"We heard the report too," said Grace. "But it doesn't start until six o'clock tonight, right?"

"That's right, Grace." Dad opened the fridge and saw that they were running low on quite a few things. "Before the weather gets too bad out there, I think it might be a good idea to make a trip to the grocery store."

"We're out of bread," said Eli, with his nose still in his book.

"And milk," said Grace, making her brother wait to flip the page. "And apples."

"And cereal."

"And mac-and-cheese."

"Exactly my point." Dad checked the emergency supply drawer in the kitchen. "We're also running low on our emergency supplies. Like batteries, in case the power goes out."

Flick.

As soon as he spoke, the lights in the house flickered. Thankfully, they stayed on.

Dad jiggled the car keys.

Eli and Grace's ears perked up. They'd waited patiently while their dad talked on the phone, caught up on his work, then paid some bills online. Now it was already three o'clock.

"If you two still want to go to Uncle Larry's store," said Dad. "We'll have to go before—"

Whoosh!

Eli and Grace jumped off the couch so fast that Dad had to jump out of the way, or else get knocked over.

"Wait! Where are you going?" Dad was already putting on his shoes and jacket.

"To get ready!" hollered Eli as he dashed up the stairs to get changed. "We can't go out dressed like this."

"Yeah, we can't go to Uncle Larry's in our pajamas!" said Grace, racing behind her brother. "You too, Dad!"

Dad looked down. "Oh. Right." He looked a bit odd wearing a bright raincoat, black dress shoes, and his favorite pair of silk blue pajamas.

All three of them were properly dressed and back downstairs in less than five minutes.

"Are we ready?" Dad held the car keys in one hand, and a large black umbrella in the other.

Eli and Grace said, "Ready!"

But one look outside was enough to give them second thoughts.

BOOM.

Thunder rumbled across the sky. It looked like the severe weather might show up sooner than six o'clock this evening.

The storm was already here.

2
Power Outage

While standing in the checkout line at the grocery store, Eli and Grace wondered if there was still time to go to Uncle Larry's store. They'd spent a lot of time shopping, so they knew it had to be getting late.

Dad checked his cell phone. "It's getting close to five o'clock already," he said. "Looks like we won't have time for a trip to Uncle Larry's store today."

Eli and Grace were disappointed, but they understood. Being safe during severe weather was more important than a trip to Uncle Larry's store. They could always go at another time.

"After this, we'll head home, okay?" said Dad. "Unless this checkout line moves a lot faster."

Click.

A checkout light came on. Then a store employee said, "I can help the next person!"

The line moved much quicker, even with so many people out buying extra supplies. Almost every shopping cart had batteries, canned food, and lots of bottled water.

"Done!" cheered Eli when the last grocery bag was loaded into the back of the SUV. All three of them were soaked from the rain, but back in the car at 4:58 p.m.

"Is there still time?" asked Eli.

Dad started the car and checked the clock on the dashboard. "Well, it takes about ten minutes to get to Uncle Larry's from here. And remember, the store closes at five-thirty. That doesn't leave much time for a proper visit. I'm sure the paddles for the inflatable kayak can wait a little while longer. How about we go some other time? We were just at Uncle Larry's store last week!"

Eli put his hands together, begging.

"*Pleeeeease*," said Grace.

"What about emergency pet food?" suggested Eli. "The fish in our aquarium might need emergency supplies to get through the storm."

"He's right, Dad," said Grace, teaming up with her brother. "The fish are part of our family too."

Dad smiled because he knew how silly they were being. Finally, he agreed. "Oh, all right, we can go," he told them. "As long as we're back at the house by six o'clock. Deal?"

"Deal," they both said.

Dad pulled out of the parking spot, quietly laughing to himself because he'd just thought of something funny.

"What's so funny, Dad?" asked Eli.

"Oh, I was just thinking how it seems strange that Uncle Larry's store really does have everything," said Dad. "His store must be the only place where you can buy a used car from the junkyard, all kinds of antiques, and fish food."

"And paddles," said Eli.

"Yeah, we might need some paddles to row our way home," said Dad, waiting for his turn to pull out into the road. Instead of turning on his left blinker, which would take them back home, he turned on his right blinker and headed for Broadway Street.

Splash!

The SUV went through another huge puddle on their way to Uncle Larry's store. There were no people out walking, and hardly any cars on the road, so they made good time driving down the usually busy roads.

Instead of listening to music like they normally did, Dad kept the radio tuned to the weather channel. The news reporter kept saying that the weather would turn nasty around six o'clock. But in some places, things had already become dangerous.

"High winds are causing damage across the county," said the news reporter. "Luckily, no injuries have been reported. Some fallen trees have knocked out power for over a thousand homes in the northeast part of the city…"

Dad turned off the radio so he could concentrate on the road. The rain was coming down in thick sheets. Even with the windshield wipers going full blast—*squeak-squeak, squeak-squeak*—it was hard to see through the heavy rain. They had to drive extra slow and careful, and watch out for the really deep water that could stall out their car.

They stopped at a red light.

"Uh-oh. Look." Dad pointed toward an abandoned vehicle out on the road. Somebody had attempted to drive their car through the underpass, then got stuck. Water had risen so high that they couldn't even see the tires!

"Wait. Is that a—?" Eli stuck his nose up to the window as they slowly passed the submerged car.

"What is it, Eli?" asked Grace.

"Never mind," said Eli, shaking his head. "It's just a stuffed animal. For a second, I thought that was a real cat in the back window."

"Me too," said Grace. "Then we would have to go rescue that poor kitty from the storm."

Sticking his face up to the window, Eli had just enough time to read the funny bumper sticker on the back of the flooded vehicle:

My other car is a broom!

3
Mari & Noah

"Is everyone ready to get wet?" Dad brought an umbrella big enough for three people, but it wouldn't help with the huge puddles.

"Ready," said Eli and Grace.

Huddled close together, squeezing in tight underneath the umbrella, they managed to get to the sidewalk without getting drenched. And it turned out that they weren't the only ones out shopping in the rain today.

Eli pulled the front door open just as another family was leaving Uncle Larry's store. A woman with two kids came out and stood on the sidewalk next to them.

"Thank you, young man," said the lady. Her two children were behind her, with dirty clothes, messy hair, and huge smiles on their faces.

"You're welcome," said Eli, then smiled when he saw a familiar face. "Mari! What are you doing here?"

"Hi, Eli!" said Mari, a friend from school. Her eyes were wide with excitement, like she'd just gotten off a roller coaster. "You are going to love this store. There's a man called Uncle Larry… and a junkyard…and when you step through the door…" She was talking very fast. It was obvious she'd just gotten back from a junkyard adventure.

Eli nodded. "We know all about it."

"Hi, Noah!" Grace waved at the boy standing there, who was in her class at school. "You know about this place too?"

Noah's eyes were huge. His clothes were torn and covered in leaves, and his black hair was sticking up like he'd been zapped with static electricity.

"This place is awesome!" said Noah, then he

and Grace whispered in secret.

Mrs. Plainview, their mother, did not look happy. While unfolding her umbrella, she told Eli and Grace's dad about how her kids had managed to break not one, not two, but *three* valuable antiques.

"I've never been so embarrassed," said Mrs. Plainview. "The owner, Mr. Larry, swore up and down that it was *him* that kept knocking things off the shelves. But nobody could be *that* clumsy. I offered to pay him, but he refused."

"Oh, you'd be surprised," said Dad. "Larry is quite the character. Clumsy, but lovable."

Mrs. Plainview sniffed. "And I simply don't know where these two get their imagination from," she said irritably. "All this talk about magic junk, and mountain climbing, and playing Scrabble with a dragon…" She held up her large red umbrella, collected her children underneath, then hurried across the parking lot toward their car.

"Bye, Mari!" shouted Eli.

"Bye, Noah!" hollered Grace.

When their friends from school were gone, Eli and Grace had to pull on the heavy glass door together. The wind had really picked up, making the door extra hard to open. Dad had to help too, otherwise the strong gusts might have knocked them off their feet.

Stinging rain pelted their cheeks.

Wind howled in their ears.

As much as Eli and Grace loved to go on junkyard adventures, they both agreed that it might have been safer to stay home.

4
Paddle Fan

Da-ding!

Bzzzz-zuzz-zuzz.

The antique bell above the door rang, then it quickly fizzled out. It had a new price tag on it—$7.00, marked down from $12.00.

"Who is it?" called a familiar voice. "I mean, uh—come in! We're open until five-thirty, folks."

Dad shook off the umbrella, then stuffed it inside what used to be a very nice porcelain umbrella stand, next to the front door. The umbrella stand had so many dents, chips, and cracks that it looked like it might fall apart.

Somebody had done a terrible job of trying to glue the pieces back together.

A faded price tag on the side read:

Handcrafted in Japan, 1880s
$11,500

The expensive price was scribbled out. Below it was a yellow sticky note that read:

$25.00
(sold as is)

As usual, Uncle Larry was behind the counter in the middle of the store. He was sitting on his old brown leather stool, using one finger to type something into the computer. Their dad had recently helped to install a new bookkeeping program, so Uncle Larry could keep better track of sales at the store. And it was working—sort of. Uncle Larry was mostly good at dealing with people, not computers.

"Eli! Grace!" Uncle Larry's round face broke

into a huge smile when he saw them. Then he accidentally leaned on a stamp pad, turning the bottom of his hand blue. He and their dad had to shake left hands instead of with their right.

"Hi, Larry," said Dad. "How are you? Staying dry, I hope. This rain is something else, isn't it?"

Uncle Larry raised his bushy eyebrows. "Rain?" He had a confused expression on his scruffy face. "Oh, yes! The witch did mention something about severe weather today."

Dad looked puzzled. "A witch?"

Eli and Grace were confused too.

Realizing his mistake, Uncle Larry quickly tried to come up with something to say. "Did I say witch?" He gave an uncomfortable laugh and pulled nervously at his wrinkly tie. "No, no, no. Silly me! I meant to say which, um…"

"Which story you were going to tell us," suggested Grace. "Right, Uncle Larry?"

"Yes! That's it!" cried Uncle Larry, looking relieved. "Here you go! A story in a bag—*er*, two bags."

Eli and Grace each took one of the plastic grocery bags that Uncle Larry was holding out. Their names were printed in black Sharpie on the side, in Uncle Larry's squiggly handwriting.

Eli & Grace

W.W.

Eli asked, "What's this, Uncle Larry?"

"Magic junk—*er*, magic book," said Uncle Larry, correcting himself. "Since I'll be busy helping your dad with the paddles for a little while, I thought you two might be able to go off and have a magical adventure on your own. I mean, uh…read your magic story."

Eli shook his bag.

It didn't sound like a book.

Uncle Larry said, "If that's okay with your dad, of course. He's the boss!"

Dad nodded. "Sure, that's fine, Larry." He looked all over the messy counter, but didn't see anything that looked remotely like paddles. "So where are they? They must be the quick release kind that you break apart, right? Are they in a box somewhere?"

Uncle Larry shifted uncomfortably on his leather stool. "Well, you see, the thing is…" His cheeks turned rosy. "Of course, you know how hot the summers can get. So last year, I might have borrowed some of Harvard's tools and tried to, um…use them."

Uncle Larry pointed up toward the ceiling.

Dad tilted his head to one side, trying to understand what he was looking at.

"Ah, yes, I see what you did," said Dad, giving a nod of approval. He had to put a hand up to his mouth to stop himself from laughing. "That's the first time I've ever seen paddles used in that way. It's an interesting concept, Larry."

Eli and Grace giggled when they noticed Uncle Larry's creation, spinning around, keeping a nice breeze going through the store.

A paddle fan.

"If Harvard will let us borrow his tools," said Dad, "then I'm sure we can figure out what we need to break it apart. And we're definitely going to need a ladder to reach all the way up there."

Uncle Larry jumped to his feet. "Coming right up!" He came bustling around the counter, then stopped. Scratching his stubbly chin, he added, "That is, if I can remember where I put the ladder. And Harvard's tool box…"

While Uncle Larry and their dad tried to figure out the best way to take down the "paddle fan," Eli and Grace took the opportunity to slip away. Together, they headed for the back of the store with the sign above the door:

Junkyard Adventures

5
Squawky Parrots

Next to the junkyard door was a wobbly plastic chair with a $3.00 price tag, and an antique chair that had some of Uncle Larry's do-it-yourself repairs. The original price ($1000) was marked down to $10 because it was in such bad shape. The sticky note read:

Chairs sold individually
(Or as a set)

Before they stepped through the junkyard door to begin their adventure, Eli and Grace sat down on the junky old chairs to check out what was inside their plastic bags.

"Let's see what we've got this time," said Eli as he pulled out the first magical treasure.

"A plastic fan?" said Grace.

Eli shrugged, then tested it out.

Whrrrrrrrrrr…

"Well, at least it works," said Eli. "Not very well, but I can feel a little bit of air blowing. I wonder why we need a mini fan?"

"Who knows," said Grace. "Maybe on this adventure we're going to a desert! We'll need a fan to keep cool."

"What did you get?" asked Eli.

Grace peeked inside her bag. "Oh," she said, disappointed. "Just these." She held up a fistful of old shoelaces. Some were flat cotton laces, others were round cotton. There were waxed laces, nylon laces, and paracord laces, which are used for lots of different hiking boots.

"A mini fan and a bunch of used shoelaces?" Grace wrinkled her nose. "Are you sure there's nothing else? Maybe Uncle Larry forgot to put something in there."

Eli felt around his bag. "Nope, that's all. We'll have to figure out the rest on our own." He left the bag on the antique chair (**Italy, 1830s**) and stuffed the plastic fan into his jacket pocket. Then he grabbed his sister's hand.

"Ready?" asked Eli, giving her hand a squeeze.

"Ready," said Grace.

The exact moment when they were about to step through the junkyard door, a loud noise made them both jump.

"PSSSSST!"

It sounded like a cat hissing.

When Eli and Grace spun around, they spotted Uncle Larry hiding behind a queen sized mattress set. One set was standing up straight, leaning against a junk shelf, while the other one way laying flat on the floor. Each mattress set was still wrapped in the crinkly plastic.

"Don't leave yet!" whispered Uncle Larry. "You don't have all your magic stuff!"

Eli and Grace waved him over, but Uncle Larry wouldn't come out from his hiding spot. He kept looking around the store, even up at the ceiling, as if expecting to see someone—or some*thing*—come swooping down on him.

SQUUAAAAWK!

A loud screeching sound echoed through the store. Everyone inside heard it. The squawking noises came from the two mini gargoyles they'd met during their last adventure.

"Um, Larry?" hollered Dad from the middle of the store. "What was that noise? Sounded like some kind of animal."

Uncle Larry was nervous about what to say. How would he explain two mini gargoyles living in his store? The truth would sound too bizarre, so the safest bet was to make up a story.

"Don't worry, Ben!" said Uncle Larry. "That was just my, um…" He waved his arms around, pleading for help about what to say.

Grace's eyes lit up. "Parrot," she whispered. "Tell him you have a new pet bird!"

Uncle Larry cleared his throat. "That was just my two new pets, Mo and Lem! They're a special breed of parrot from the deep, um…wilderness." He smacked his forehead, wishing he'd come up with something better to say.

The store was quiet for a moment.

"Okay, Larry!" said Dad. "I'm going to need some different screwdrivers to get these paddles off the ceiling fan. There are at least five different types of screws holding it together. And probably some sharp scissors to cut through all this duct tape."

Uncle Larry was relieved that he didn't have to explain the strange noises. "Okay, Ben! I'll find some of those screwdriver thingys, then be right there to help!"

Eli and Grace wanted to ask about their gargoyle friends, Mobius and Lemniscate, but Uncle Larry needed to get back to helping their dad take down the paddle fan.

"Don't worry about those two squawkers," said Uncle Larry. "They're both driving me up the wall, of course, but Mo and Lem are doing just fine." He let out a huge sigh, then took a moment to collect his thoughts. "Now—um, what was I talking about?"

"Our magic junk," Grace reminded him. "All we have so far is this plastic fan."

"And these," said Eli, holding several yards worth of junky old shoelaces. He was hoping for something epic, like the jeweled sword that Professor Harvard had the last time they were at the store. Their magic junk wasn't nearly as exciting as a knight's sword.

"Ah, there we are!" Uncle Larry had to search each of his pockets, but finally found what he was looking for. "Your most important piece of magic." He pulled a round metal canister from his jacket pocket and dusted it off like it was extremely valuable.

Eli and Grace couldn't tell what it was at first, but assumed it must be really important.

"Now, let's see…" Uncle Larry went back and forth between the two of them. "Which of you can be trusted to keep this special treasure safe?" He finally handed the dented can over to Grace.

"Cat food?" said Eli, unimpressed.

Grace read the label. "Made with flavors of salmon, tuna, shrimp, and seaweed." She made a face. "Sounds good…if you're a cat."

Uncle Larry laughed. "I was beginning to wonder why in the world I was walking around with a tin of cat food in my pocket all day."

"Here, Eli. Hold the shoelaces for me, please," said Grace, then handed them to her brother. "Your jacket has bigger pockets than mine."

She stuffed the can of cat food into her pocket and zipped it up. And just in case, each of them stuffed their plastic grocery bag into their jeans pocket.

"And don't forget," said Uncle Larry, already heading down the aisle. "Remember to work together. And once you begin—"

"We have to finish," said Eli and Grace.

Uncle Larry gave them a thumbs-up, then hurried off to help their dad with the paddle fan.

Eli reached out his hand.

Creeeeeeak!

The junkyard door opened all by itself.

Neither of them could tell if they were looking out at the magical world of junkyard adventures or just the regular outside, gray and miserable.

"What's out there?" asked Grace.

"I don't know," said Eli. "It's too dark to tell."

When they stepped through the door—

Whoosh!

They were gone.

6
Quiet Nights & Bright City Lights

No stars were visible in the sky. Above them was only a mix of gray and black clouds—same as back home. Thunder rumbled in the distance. There were no houses, no buildings, and no vehicles on the road. Just the road.

"Where are we?" asked Eli, waiting for his eyes to adjust to the dark. "I can hardly see anything but the yellow lines beneath our feet."

Hills rose up on either side, spreading out for miles. Behind them was nothing but inky black.

"We're in the middle of the road somewhere," said Grace, searching for any kind of sign or direction marker.

"More like the middle of nowhere," said Eli. "But at least it's not raining."

"Yeah, not yet," said Grace, looking worried.

More thunder growled high in the sky. If they didn't find shelter soon, they'd be stuck out in the rain, during a severe storm.

For a minute or two, they stood around and waited for something to happen. Anything to give them some kind of clue.

Nothing was out here—except *them*.

"Come on," said Eli, taking his sister's hand. "We're standing in the middle of the road. We better move before a car comes along."

With nothing but a spooky darkness behind them, the only option was to walk along the shoulder and follow the yellow lines on the road.

They hadn't been walking for very long before a sign appeared. It was too dark to read it from a distance, but they could tell something else was there too. Leaning up against the wooden post of the road sign were two metal shapes, each with light reflectors and glow-in-the-dark wheels.

"Are those—?" Eli had to squint his eyes in the dark. "That looks like a couple of racing scooters."

"Yeah, you're right," said Grace. "Just like the ones we have at home."

Jogging toward the road sign, they discovered they were both right.

"Not just scooters," said Eli, grabbing hold of the one with the bright green handlebars. "These are *our* scooters—from home."

Eli's scooter had neon green wheels and stickers all over. Grace's scooter had some LED lights and a silver bell.

Brrrring!

Eli flinched. "Yeah, that's definitely your scooter," he said, making a face. "It has that loud, annoying bell."

Grace rang the bell again just to tease him. "What does the sign say?" She tried to make out the letters in the dark. "Weather…something."

Weatherville
1 Mile

"Grace, look!" Eli pointed beyond the sign, where a huge hill went down, down, down. And way at the bottom were a ton of bright, shining lights—city lights.

Just not *their* city.

7
Flood Street

Flying down the hill at night was amazing! The streetlights made it easier to see in the dark. It also helped them to avoid crashing into each other as they raced down the long stretch of smooth pavement.

Eli crouched down on his scooter to go even faster, while Grace stood up tall and allowed the wind to whip through her long hair.

"This is great!" Eli shouted over his shoulder. "Are you okay back there?"

Brrrring!

Grace rang her bell to let him know she was

right behind him. "Yes, I'm okay! Just be careful up there! You don't want to crash."

When the road finally leveled out, they lost all their speed. They pushed along on their scooters until their legs were tired, then rolled to a stop and walked for a while.

Soon they came across another sign.

Flood Street

"Usually the main road through downtown is called Main Street," said Eli. "But I guess Flood Street works too. I just hope the street doesn't actually get flooded."

A few cars were parked in the street, but there were no people around. No shoppers peeking in the storefront windows, no shopkeepers talking to customers, and no sign of life.

"The whole town must be asleep," said Grace.

As they walked past the decorated windows, Eli and Grace read the names of all the shops and boutiques. Most stores had a funny name: *The Conjuring Café*, *Mystic Laundromat*, *Alchemy*

Books & Gifts, and one called *Soothsaying Supply Store*.

"All these stores look fun," said Grace, pushing her scooter alongside her brother. "I'd like to visit them if we have time."

"I would too," said Eli. "But none of them are open for business. I wonder what time it is here?"

The streetlights were on, and the small trees lining the sidewalk all had strings of lights, so the main road through town was well lit.

As they kept walking, Eli commented that the storm was probably the reason why nobody else was around.

It was already starting to rain.

"Any ideas?" asked Eli as they walked by the last few shops on Flood Street. They must have passed at least a dozen stores, but all they came across were a lot of **CLOSED** signs hanging on the doors and windows.

"Maybe this is a shopping adventure," suggested Grace. "We've never done that before."

"Can't be," said Eli. "It's nighttime. And the stores are all closed. Every single one of them."

The sidewalk ended abruptly. It was too dark to tell what was out there, past the edge of town.

"I guess that's it," said Eli. "No more stores, no more streetlights. Maybe we should go back."

"Yeah, maybe," said Grace, sounding unsure. She kept thinking they were missing something, or overlooking an important detail.

"Who knows what's out that way," said Eli, peering out into the darkness. "Could be giant spiders, or slimy snakes, or—never mind." He stopped because he didn't want to scare his sister—or *himself*. He also didn't want to let on that he was getting nervous about standing around too long in a place called Flood Street.

"Well, we can't just hang out here all night," said Grace, standing close to her brother. "We have to figure out this adventure. I don't want to spend the night in the dark."

"Me neither," said Eli. "We don't have any

camping gear like on our last adventure."

Although they'd been gone for a while, nobody had shown up to help or offer assistance. There were no helpful monsters, or giants, or dragons—no teacher of any kind. Just them and their scooters, in a strange town, at night, with a thunderstorm on the way.

Grace tapped her brother on the shoulder, since he hadn't noticed it yet.

"There's a light on," she said. "Look! Up there."

"Oh yeah," said Eli. "I see it—barely."

A short hike from where Flood Street ended, a lonely hill rose high above downtown Weatherville. Sitting on top of the hill was an old house at least four stories high. Boards covered the windows, and there were holes in the roof. The entire house seemed to be leaning heavily to one side.

But still, the lights were on.

"Should we go see if anyone's home?" asked Grace. "That house must be there for a reason."

Eli wasn't so sure they should leave such a well-lit area. He didn't want to seem afraid in front of his sister, but he *was* afraid. The house on the hill looked spooky. Maybe even haunted.

"We'll go together," said Grace. "Deal?"

Eli reluctantly agreed. "Deal," he said. "We can't ride our scooters uphill, so I guess we'll carry them."

With the simple push of a release button, their scooters folded in half, making them much easier to carry.

Together, in the dark, they walked up the hill toward the old, crooked house.

A witch's house.

8
Doll House

After a long hike up the hill, Eli and Grace were breathing hard by the time they reached the top. They set their scooters next to the railing outside the house, then walked up the creaky front porch steps.

Squeak, squeak.

From a distance, the house looked like a place you would only visit on a dare. Maybe on Halloween night, to see which of your friends was brave enough to ring the doorbell.

Spinning around on the tip-top of the roof was a *weather vane*, an instrument used to show the direction of the wind. This was the strangest weather vane either of them had ever seen. It was shaped like an umbrella. Just underneath the umbrella-vane were four pointy metal letters:

N, S, E, W

Many of the wooden boards holding the house together had already fallen off, while others were just barely hanging on by a nail or two. And all the windows were boarded up—except for one room up on the top floor, which had a light on.

The front door looked like Uncle Larry made it himself, using old wood and rusty hinges.

"Well?" said Grace.

"Well what?" replied Eli. "I'm not going in there. This place gives me the creeps."

They both had a feeling this was the right place, it was just that neither of them wanted to go first. Dark curtains were pulled across the windows, so they couldn't see inside.

"Should we knock?" asked Grace, standing safely behind her brother.

"Go ahead," Eli said. "Try it."

Grace shook her head. "No way," she said. "You're the oldest, so you have to knock."

Eli sighed. "Oh, all right. One quick knock, and then we're leaving, okay?" He reached out his trembling hand, and suddenly—

Creeeeeeeak.

The front door opened all on its own.

Eli stuck his nose just past the threshold of the door. "Hello? Is anyone home?"

Taking a deep breath, Grace said, "Sorry about this, Eli!" Then she shoved him through the doorway and into the house. She hurried in after him, so he wouldn't get mad.

"Don't do that!" said Eli. "You scared me."

"Sorry," she said. "But we have to do *something*. We can't just stand around all night. What if Dad's looking for us already?"

"Yes, I know…" whispered Eli. "But no more pushing and shoving. Uncle Larry says we're supposed to work as a team, remember?"

"Yes, I remember," Grace told him. "But why are you whispering? There's nobody here. The place is empty. And look! This house isn't so scary."

Small glowing orbs were placed on the tables. They gave off enough light to explore without crashing into anything.

Eli had to agree with his sister. "From the outside, this place looks kind of scary," he said, taking a few more cautious steps. "But the inside is really nice."

Chandeliers hung from the ceiling. Candelabras with long white candles were placed on the table, the mantel, and a dozen other places. And the solid oak bookshelf was crammed full of hardcover books, some of which had to be hundreds of years old.

"Pretty clean for a haunted house," said Eli.

The hardwood floors looked like they'd been polished recently. And the black-and-gold area rug looked like it might have come from Uncle Larry's store. In fact, all the dusty furniture—from the paw-footed couch with gold trim to the fancy table and chairs—looked like it could have come from Uncle Larry's store.

Eli cupped his hands to his mouth and hollered, "HELLO! Is anyone here?"

The house remained silent.

Outside, the wind continued to howl. The bigger gusts blew so hard they rattled the windows and doors.

"Should we go upstairs?" Eli had one hand on the carved wooden rail, and one foot on the bottom step. But he just stood there, waiting.

Grace slipped her hand inside Eli's. "Don't worry," she told him. "I'll go with you."

"Ha! You better come too," said Eli, grinning. "This was *your* idea, remember? I wanted to stay back in town. At least we were safe back there."

Squeak, squeak.

The steps going up to the second floor creaked louder than the front porch. If anybody was home, they definitely heard the noise.

Soon they were standing in front of the room with the yellow glow coming from inside. A thin strip of light was visible from the gap between the door and the squeaky hardwood floor.

"Hello?" Eli politely knocked. "Is anyone in there? We could use a little help, or maybe some directions. My sister and I are stranded here."

When no response came, Eli turned the antique glass door knob and slowly pushed open the door.

It was a bedroom.

A cracked mirror hung on one wall, and a broken picture frame—with no picture—hung on the opposite wall. The flowered wallpaper had faded from its original gold color to a tarnished yellow, and most of it was peeling off.

The only other thing in the room was a fancy wooden bed, just big enough for a child. The headboard and footboard were carved with designs of crescent moons, stars, and tall pointed hats. Propped up on the frilly, decorative pillows was the only toy in the room.

A doll.

"See? There's nothing scary in here," said

Grace, stroking the doll's curly hair. She was admiring its colorful striped socks, beautiful purple dress, and the detail of its porcelain face when the doll did something unexpected.

"What's wrong?" asked Eli.

Grace screamed when the doll began to shudder and tremble in her hand.

"Here, take it!" cried Grace, holding the vibrating doll at arm's length.

Eli jumped back. "I don't want it. Throw it back on the bed!"

Grace did exactly what Eli suggested. She tossed the shaking doll back onto the bed, but it was too late. She had already touched the doll, and that was enough to spark the magic spell.

Poof!

There was a burst of light, then a cloud of smoke filled the bedroom. It wasn't the kind of smoke that made you cough, just the kind that made it hard to see.

"A-ha!" said a lady's voice. "Children, I see!"

It was too late to run.

When the cloud of purple smoke cleared, they saw a woman standing next to the bed. She had long, frizzy hair, striped socks, and her feet weren't touching the ground.

She was clearly a witch.

9
Emergency List

The witch spun around in the air, laughing and singing to herself. She flopped back down, sat on the edge of the bed, and watched them closely.

"It's good to be back in my old room again," said the witch. "I grew up in this house, you know. Lived here my whole life, ever since I was just a wee little witch."

Eli shook his head. "Um, no. We didn't know that," he said, trying to protect his sister. "Sorry about coming into your house without being invited. We'll just leave now. Bye!"

The witch sprang to her feet, though her shiny

black shoes never actually touched the ground.

"You can't leave," she said. "Not until you're done with this." She handed them a list.

Severe Weather Checklist

1) Prepare emergency kit: food, water, batteries, flashlight, radio, first-aid kit.
2) Close windows and doors.
3) Unplug electrical devices.
4) Find a safe place.

After Eli and Grace finished reading the list, they finally realized that the old house, the empty town, and the witchy woman were all a part of their junkyard adventure.

"I'm here to guide you on your way to severe weather safety," said the witch. "My students sometimes call me the weather witch. But my friends call me Misty."

Grace raised her hand as if they were in a classroom. "Misty, can you help us?"

"Of course!" said Misty. "That's what teachers do! They help their students."

Eli's mouth fell open. "You're a teacher?" He felt better knowing this, even though he'd never met a real witch before.

Misty gave a shrill laugh. "Ah, you might be surprised, Eli. There are lots of witches out there. But most of them don't go around telling others about their special witchy talents."

BOOM.

Thunder exploded outside. It was so loud that it shook the whole house.

"That sounded close," said Eli as he rushed to the window. He pulled back the curtain and saw bright flashes of lightning tearing across the sky. The house was creaking from the wind.

"The storm is more than just *close*, Eli," said the weather witch. "It's already here! Thunder, lightning, and high winds." She sounded excited. "That means we—that is, *you two*—only have a few minutes to find what you need."

While checking over the list again, the sounds of the storm grew louder. Eli and Grace both realized this wasn't a trick. A terrible storm really was on the way. Their family didn't have a severe weather plan, or a checklist, so they weren't sure where to start.

Misty held up one finger. "Now remember, if you hear a loud noise that goes *beep-beep-beeeeeeeep!* That'll be the warning buzzer for the dam. It's old and crumbly, but still holding on."

Eli's face turned pale. "This town has a dam?"

Grace's mouth suddenly went dry. "Eli, you know I'm not a good swimmer yet. I'm still in swimming lessons!"

Misty spun in the air. "If the dam breaks, then the entire town will be flooded. Now you know why I built my house on top of the hill!" She cackled. "But if you hear a sound that goes *rooooo-rooooo!* That'll be the tornado siren."

Eli and Grace were beginning to panic. Now it was *them* circling around the room, not the witch.

"What do we do?" said Eli, waving his arms.

"Where do we go?" shouted Grace.

The weather witch tried her best to calm them down, telling her new students to focus on their task.

"First, you have to find everything on that list," Misty reminded them. "Those are the emergency items you'll need. When that's done, you must get to safety. There is a storm cellar around the side of the house. It's dark and a bit spooky, but at least you'll be safe down there."

Eli took a few deep breaths. "Okay, calm down," he told himself. "Find the things on the list, then get to the storm cellar. Got it. Are you ready, Grace?"

"Ready," said Grace. "I think so…?"

Ka-BOOM.

Thunder rattled the house.

The weather witch was flying through the air again, zooming around in circles like this was a party. She was the only one who seemed thrilled that a storm was on the way.

"Wake me when it's over!" said Misty, waving goodbye. "And remember, tornadoes can travel in any direction. So the storm may blow right past this area. But if you see hail…watch out! After that comes the sound of a roaring freight train. That'll be the tornado dropping out of the sky."

Eli remembered something their dad sometimes says: *the calm before the storm*.

Misty the weather witch cackled again. She rose into the air, saying, "Bye for now, Eli and Grace! Be safe, and work together. Good luck!"

"Misty, wait!" said Eli. "How do we—"

Poof!

With a flash of white light and a puff of purple smoke, the weather witch was gone. She didn't leave the house, or even the room. She'd turned back into a doll—a weather witch doll, laying on the pillow, just like how they'd found her.

Grace leaned over the bed, staring into the eyes of the doll. "Misty? Are you in there? Ms. Weather Witch, can you hear me?"

Eli pulled her away from the doll. "Come on, Grace. You heard what the weather witch told us. We need to finish this emergency list—*fast*. Then we have to find the storm shelter."

10
Flying Flashlight

After quickly dividing up the emergency list, Eli and Grace raced off in different directions. Grace got busy working on the first item on the list.

1) Prepare emergency kit: food, water, batteries, flashlight, radio, first-aid kit.

Every cupboard in the kitchen was stuffed with canned foods, dried foods, and snack foods. Grace made a large pile on the counter, then searched for water. The fridge didn't have any food, but on the bottom shelf was a brand-new package of bottled water. She grabbed as many bottles as she thought the plastic bag could hold, then hurried off in search of the first-aid kit.

Eli was busy working on the second item on their emergency list.

2) Close windows and doors.

He rushed around the first floor of the house, working as quickly as he could. The doors were easy to close, but the locks on the windows were antique *sash* locks—the kind of lock shaped like a half-circle, and require a half-turn to open and close. But the house was so old that hardly any of the locks lined up properly. So it took him extra time to close all the windows.

"Got it!" Grace came running into the living room holding a small white box. "Eli, I found a first-aid kit in the bathroom. How's it going with the doors and windows?"

Click.

"Done!" said Eli, securing the last window. "All the windows and doors are closed. What's next?"

"We still need a flashlight," said Grace, reading over the list. "And extra batteries."

Without a moment to waste, they ran to the kitchen and kept working on the list. The rain was really coming down hard. And the wind was picking up too. They were both worried that they'd hear the sound of a siren at any second.

"Okay, I've got food and water ready to go," said Grace. "But we need another bag to carry it all. Do you still have the one Uncle Larry gave you? The one with your magic junk?"

"Yeah, right here." Eli handed her the plastic bag he'd stuffed into his pocket. He was glad that he'd kept it, instead of leaving the bag at Uncle Larry's store.

"You finish packing and I'll find a flashlight," said Eli, already searching through the kitchen drawers with the peeling white paint.

Thunk.

"Empty."

Clunk.

"Nothing."

Eli kept checking drawer after drawer, but couldn't find what they needed. He checked the bottom cupboards, highest shelves, and even on top of the fridge.

"The food and water is all packed and ready to go," said Grace. "You keep looking for the flashlight. I'm going to start searching for a radio."

Ka-BOOM.

More thunder.

"Yes!" cheered Eli when he found exactly what they needed. "Grace, I found the flashlight!" He pocketed the package of black-and-gold batteries, then reached into the drawer to grab the flashlight. But the flashlight didn't stay in the drawer. It floated away—like *magic*.

"Hey!" shouted Eli. "Get back here!"

Grace came back a moment later, empty-handed. She discovered her brother running back and forth, yelling and chasing after a flying flashlight.

"Eli, stop goofing around!" warned Grace. "We need to get down to the storm cellar."

"I'm not goofing around," said Eli, jumping and missing again. "This flashlight is bonkers!"

Grace crossed her arms. "This is a witch's house, remember? So things may act a little funny."

"Ha! Gotcha!" Eli was finally able to sneak up behind the flying flashlight, then grab it when it was pointed the other way.

"We have another problem," said Grace.

"What is it?"

"I can't find a radio anywhere," she said, her eyes filled with worry. "I checked everywhere downstairs, but there isn't one. Should we go look upstairs?"

Slam.

The front door suddenly blew open, making them both jump. Then another sound cut through the air. It was the same sound the weather witch had warned them about.

Rooooo-rooooo!

The tornado siren was going off.

11

Run for Cover

Eli grabbed the heavy grocery bag from the kitchen, while Grace took one more fast look around the living room, searching for the one thing they still needed from the list.

"We're still missing the radio," shouted Grace. It was difficult to hear over the noise of the storm.

"There's no time!" shouted Eli. "We have to get to the storm cellar! Now!"

Rooooo-rooooo!

The tornado siren continued to wail. Wind blew so fiercely that it shook the entire house. Neither of them had experienced anything like it.

They only had a few minutes to get to safety.

Halfway to the front door, Eli stopped.

Outside was eerily still. Then came a soft noise, like pebbles rolling off the roof.

"What is it?" asked Grace. "What's wrong?"

"Shhh," said Eli. "Listen."

Tink-tink.

Tink-tink-tink-tink-tink!

The noise was gentle at first, but quickly became so loud that it sounded like baseballs were hitting the roof.

"What's that sound?" asked Grace, who was too young to remember their last hailstorm.

"Oh no," Eli groaned. "It's hailing."

Then came a roar like a freight train.

"Hold tight and don't let go!" Eli grabbed his sister by the hand. They hurried out the front door, down the steps, and around the side of the house. Both of them nearly panicked when they made it to one side and found nothing there.

"Other side!" shouted Eli, pointing to the opposite side of the house.

The wind nearly knocked them off their feet as they ran. Debris was also another concern, but so far they were okay. The noise was incredible! It sounded like a *hundred* freight trains, all of them racing across the sky with their horns blasting.

"I see it!" cried Grace.

The cellar door was too big and awkward for Eli to open by himself. No matter how hard he pulled, the old wooden door was too heavy to lift.

"Move over!" said Grace. "Let me help!"

Although it was still a struggle with two pairs of strong arms, lifting and pulling, they finally managed to get one side of the door open.

"Hurry!" yelled Eli. "Get inside!"

Grace slipped past her brother and stood on an old wooden staircase. It was so dark that she couldn't tell how far down the stairs went.

"Pass me the emergency bags!" said Grace, reaching out her arms. She placed their emergency supplies on the steps, then helped her brother get inside the storm shelter.

Once they were both standing on the staircase, Eli said, "Okay, we're in. But how are we going to shut the cellar—"

Bang!

"—door," finished Eli. "Never mind. I guess the wind took care of it."

Now they were trapped.

12
The Cellar

Fumbling around in the dark was dangerous. But once Eli got the flashlight working, they both felt better. The dirt floor wasn't very comfortable to sit on, but the walls were made of thick cement, so at least they were safe from the storm.

A few rickety wooden shelves lined the walls. They were loaded with black cauldrons of all different sizes, candles made from glass jars, and many other dusty old antiques that hadn't been touched in years.

Shadows were everywhere.

Grace shivered. "It's spooky down here," she said. "Even with the flashlight."

Eli agreed. "Yeah, but at least we're safe from the storm," he said, shaking off the cold. "Being down here is a lot better than being up there, where the walls—or the entire house—might be destroyed."

In the distance, another siren began to wail.

Beep! Beep! Beeeeeeeep!

"That must be the warning siren for the dam the weather witch told us about," said Eli. "I hope it holds up."

"Me too," said Grace. "Otherwise the town of Weatherville will be a giant swimming pool."

Somewhere above, the house was taking a beating from the fierce winds.

Down in the cellar, the only thing they could do was wait out the storm.

BOOM.

An explosion made them jump. This was followed by the sound of rushing water—a *lot* of rushing water.

"I hope that wasn't the dam breaking," said Eli, though he couldn't think of what else would make such a noise. The tornado siren was still blaring, but the second alarm—the dam warning—had suddenly stopped.

"I hope everything's okay up there," said Grace. "Do you think the weather witch's house is still in one piece?"

Eli shrugged. "I don't know," he said. "I'd be more worried about Flood Street. The weather witch's house should be okay since it's up on a hill. But all those shops and stores we passed are down at the bottom of the hill."

"So this is probably the safest place, right?" asked Grace, her eyes wide and fearful.

"Of course," said Eli, gently patting her shoulder. "I just hope the storm doesn't last too long."

To take their minds off the terrible weather, Eli passed out snacks and bottles of water.

By the time they finished their snack, each of them enjoying a small bag of plain potato chips, the storm had quieted down.

"Is it over?" asked Grace.

Eli got up off the floor to check. "Hey, at least we don't have to worry about lifting the heavy cellar door."

Half of the door was missing.

"The wind must have pulled it off the hinges," said Eli. He stuck his head outside and took a good look around. It was still dark, but now he could see the stars shining above.

"Is it safe?" asked Grace.

"I think it's okay," said Eli. "There's no rain, no wind, or anything bad going on outside. I think the storm has passed."

Everything happened so quickly that it was all very exciting. It was thrilling to rush through the house in search of emergency supplies, then go racing down to the storm cellar. But really, the whole experience was *frightening*, not thrilling. Neither of them had ever been this close to severe weather.

"I know one thing," said Eli, coming back down the steps to help his sister pick up their things.

"What?" asked Grace.

"I'll never look at a storm the same way again," said Eli. "I've seen lots of thunderstorms, but never anything like that." He paused. "Wait a second—"

"What is it?" asked Grace.

"Hey, look what I found!" Eli held up a small red box. "It's exactly what we need!"

When he shined the flashlight toward the far shelf, a small red box caught his attention. All this time he'd been keeping an eye out for something similar to the one they had back home, with big speakers, and a plug for electricity. But this was the kind that used a hand crank to give it power.

A wind up radio.

"We finished the list!" cheered Grace. She wrapped her arms around her brother and squeezed him so hard he begged to be let go.

"Come on," said Eli. "Let's get out of the storm shelter and find the weather witch. She's the only one who can help us get back to Uncle Larry's."

After collecting the emergency supplies, and picking up their trash, they walked up the wooden staircase and out of the storm cellar.

Dark gray thunderclouds still hung in the night sky, but now they could see the moon peeking through. Lightning flashed and thunder rumbled in the distance, but the storm was moving away!

"Eli, look! The weather witch's house is still standing," said Grace. "I didn't think it would survive the storm."

"Yeah, but look down there," said Eli. He pointed down the hill, where all the water from the dam had ended up.

Flood Street was flooded.

13
Small Favors

Back in the weather witch's room, the frame with no picture had fallen off the wall. Everything else seemed okay, though. The cracked mirror was still hanging by its nail, and the doll—a miniature version of the weather witch—was still on the bed.

"Should I wake her up?" asked Grace, standing over the doll.

"Yeah, I guess we have to wake her up during each visit," said Eli. "Just remember what happened last time." He hung the picture back up on the wall, while Grace tried to bring the doll to life.

"Ms. Weather Witch? Are you in there?" Grace didn't want to pick the doll up. Instead, she pushed down on the mattress with both hands and gently shook the bed. "Misty? Come awake if you can hear me."

Nothing happened, so she carefully reached out her hand. As soon as the tip of her finger touched the fabric of the doll, it began to shake. Then it stood up and danced on the bed. The room crackled with energy, like static electricity. And with a burst of purple smoke—

Poof!

The weather witch was back.

"Is the storm over already?" asked Misty. "Did you complete the list? Are you both okay?" She was thrilled to be back with her two new students.

Eli and Grace were glad to see her too. They just wished the weather witch's sudden appearances weren't quite so dramatic.

"Yes, we're fine," Eli told the witch. "And we finished everything on the checklist. See?" He held up his grocery bag, showing off their emergency supplies. And Grace held up her bag with the radio and first-aid kit.

Misty was so delighted that she spun around in circles, flailing her arms, and sending purple sparks across the room. Then she produced a ballpoint pen that looked at lot like the ones from Uncle Larry's store.

"Mm-hm, mm-hm," said the witch, checking to make sure they got everything. "Excellent work, both of you. That was only a *magical* storm— created by me, of course. But you can imagine how important it is to get to safety whenever there's a *real* storm."

Eli and Grace agreed.

"So…is that it?" asked Eli, disappointed.

"Is our adventure over?" asked Grace.

The weather witch walked back and forth across the room, though her shiny black boots never touched the floor.

"Actually, my dears, " said Misty, tapping her chin. "There is one small favor I must ask of you."

Zap!

From the tips of her fingers, the weather witched produced a shower of purple sparks. She aimed them at the empty painting on the far wall. When Eli and Grace turned to look this time, the canvas wasn't empty any longer.

It was a painting of a cat.

A black cat.

"That's my friendly feline," said Misty, keeping the trail of sparks going by wiggling her fingers. "His name is Smokey. I've had him since I was just a little witch. He's almost as old as I am!"

Fssst!

When the weather witch released the spell, the picture faded and became a blank canvas once again.

"Most days he stays inside the painting," explained Misty. "But today he seems to have wandered off. Do you mind going to look for him? It's awfully close to dinnertime, so he must be getting hungry."

Eli looked at Grace, then back at the weather witch. They were both thinking the same thing.

"Do we have time?" asked Eli.

"Dad might be looking for us," said Grace. "Or is he still helping Uncle Larry?"

The witch's face brightened. "Excellent question," she said. "Why don't we take a little peek!" With another wiggle of her fingers, more sparks shot out. Gold sparks this time, and they were aimed at the cracked mirror on the wall.

Zap!

In the mirror, a cloudy image swirled around and around. When it stopped moving, the hidden scene was revealed. They were all peering into Uncle Larry's store.

"It's Dad!" said Grace as she and her brother stuck their faces up close.

"Uh-oh," said Eli. "Looks like they've already taken down three fan blades. There's only one more left."

Zap!

The witch released the spell and the image was gone. It was just a cracked mirror again.

"As you can see, there is still enough time to find my cat," said Misty, floating around the room. "If you find him quickly enough, then perhaps I can take you on a storm tour."

Eli and Grace thought that sounded fun.

"Where do we start?" asked Eli. "Could Smokey be hiding in the house somewhere?"

"Or in the backyard?" suggested Grace.

The weather witch shook her head. "No, I'm afraid Smokey likes to wander around town while I'm teaching my classes. He likes to snoop around the shops. Especially the pet store."

Eli gulped. "Flood Street?"

Grace grabbed his hand. "Don't worry, Misty," she told the friendly witch. "We'll find your cat."

The weather witch smiled. "Oh! That reminds me—" More sparks shot out. "Could you also keep an eye out for my umbrella? I seem to have lost it. I'm afraid my magic umbrella is the only way I can take you back to Uncle Larry's store."

Eli was beginning to get worried. Their list kept getting longer, and there wasn't much time.

"Rescue a cat, search for an umbrella…" Eli let out a heavy sigh. "Is there anything else we need to do?"

The weather witch pointed to the grocery bags on the floor. "Before you go, could you put all the emergency supplies back where you found them, please? That way, they'll be ready for the next kids."

Eli and Grace agreed to put everything back where they'd found it. It was exciting to know that other kids could go on this same stormy adventure.

"But keep the plastic bags," said Misty. "You may need them."

Poof!

With another blast of smoke, the weather witch was gone, leaving them alone in the room.

"Ready?" asked Eli.

"Ready," said Grace.

Each of them grabbed a grocery bag, then hurried downstairs. There was still a lot to do, and not a lot of time to do it.

14
Smokey on the Water

After the emergency supplies were put back in their proper spots, and the radio was replaced in the storm cellar, Eli and Grace hurried down the hill. They stood on the edge of a huge lake, right where the shopping district had been.

Eli shined the flashlight across the water. All he could see were lots of shapes and shadows. The shops were under at least four feet of water. Only the roofs of the cars parked in the street were visible. The whole town was submerged.

"Smokey could be anywhere," said Eli. "How

are we ever going to find a black cat in the dark? And besides, I thought cats don't like to swim."

A soft noise cut through the air.

Meow.

Grace tapped her brother on the shoulder to get his attention. "Eli, shine the flashlight this way. Smokey is over there. See him? He's right there, staring at us."

Eli shined the flashlight up and down Flood Street, until the beam picked up a small, dark shape sitting on the roof of a flooded car. The light reflected in the cat's yellow-green eyes.

Meow.

"Okay, we found the cat," said Eli. "But how are we supposed to get way over there? We need a boat to rescue him."

Again, Eli felt a tap on his shoulder.

"Um, Eli? We do have a boat," said Grace, then dragged her brother over toward the folded shape laying in the wet grass.

It wasn't exactly a boat, but close.

An inflatable kayak.

"Is that ours?" Eli kneeled down to help his sister unfold the synthetic rubber kayak and spread it out.

"Yeah, it's ours," said Grace. "It's the same one Dad bought the other day at Uncle Larry's store."

Meow.

Smokey kept calling to them.

Working as a team, Eli used the foot pump to inflate the kayak, while Grace kept hold of the air nozzle. It took only a few minutes until the kayak was ready for a cat rescue.

"Uh-oh," said Grace.

"What's wrong?" Eli was feeling good, so he hoped his sister didn't have more bad news.

Grace searched everywhere in the wet grass, but came up empty-handed.

"We don't have any paddles," she told him. "They're back at the store, remember? Dad is taking them off of Uncle Larry's paddle fan right now."

Eli let out a sigh. "The wind will just blow us off course," he said, sounding defeated. "We'll never be able to make it down Flood Street." In frustration, he meant to smack his leg, but instead his hand caught on his jacket pocket.

"Wait a second—?" Eli's eyes lit up. Without an explanation, he shoved the kayak into the water and got in. Then he reached out a hand to help Grace step inside the wobbly watercraft.

"We don't have paddles…" Eli was holding something in his hand. "But I'll bet we can use this!" He held up the magic item that Uncle Larry had given him.

The plastic fan.

When he turned it on, the fan didn't do much. Eli could barely feel it pushing any air around. The moment he plunged his hand into the water—

Whrrrrrrrrrr…

The kayak took off like a motorboat!

"Grace, hold on!" cried Eli, trying to keep the boat steady. "This motor-fan really works!"

Using the magic fan to speed down Flood Street, they reached Smokey the cat in no time. Now they faced a different kind of problem.

"Smokey, come on, will you? *Pleeease*?" Grace tried everything she could think of to get the cat to jump into the kayak. Nothing worked. The cat simply stared at her with its yellow-green eyes that seemed to glow in the dark. She whistled, patted her lap, and even tried to get the cat to chase the beam of the flashlight.

Smokey just stood there, looking bored.

Meow.

"I give up," said Grace. "Every time I try to grab him, he moves away."

"Maybe I can try and tempt him with the shoelaces that Uncle Larry gave me," suggested Eli. "That might get him to come aboard."

"What we really need is some—" Grace's eyes suddenly lit up like she remembered something.

"Is some what?" said Eli, waiting.

Grace was busy searching her pockets. For a moment, she was worried that she'd dropped it somewhere along the way.

Pop!

The lid came right off.

"Here, Smokey!" Grace held the "magic" item that Uncle Larry had given her. It wasn't magic, but it definitely did the trick. No cat can resist the delicious taste of salmon, tuna, shrimp, and yummy seaweed.

Eli tried to help too. "Mmm, fish and seaweed! Come on, Smokey. Dinnertime!"

Meow.

The cat could resist no longer.

"Gotcha!" cheered Grace when the cat jumped right into her lap, meowing to be fed.

"Hold him tight," said Eli. "Here we go!" He plunged his hand back into the water and the kayak took off once again.

Whrrrrrrrrrrr…

Smokey only got to finish half of his treat during the ride back. Although upset, the cat still followed the curious boy and girl with the tasty food all the way up the hill, and back to the house.

Grace ran up the squeaky porch steps with Smokey the cat close behind, ready to finish his seafood dinner.

"Eli? Are you coming?" asked Grace.

Her brother stood outside, staring up at the roof. He shined the flashlight up at the top, where the strange weather vane gently blew in the wind.

"I think I know where the weather witch's umbrella is," Eli called to his sister. "We just need to figure out how to get it."

The witch's umbrella was up at the very tip-top of the roof. There was no way to reach it. Not without an extremely tall ladder. Or maybe a hot air balloon.

15
Inflatable Eli

The moment Eli and Grace stepped through the door to the witch's room, Smokey the cat raced between their legs. With a great leap, the cat sprang into the air. There was a bright flash, then the cat was back inside the painting.

"It's a painting of this room," said Eli, sticking his nose up close to it. "There's Smokey, the bed, and the cracked mirror on the wall. And there are two kids standing right—" He tilted his head to the side. "Wait, is that—?"

Grace stood next to her brother to get a closer look at the picture. "Yep, it's us."

Behind them was the cracked mirror, which acted like a special kind of camera, to document all the kids who had this same witchy adventure.

"Okay, we rescued the cat," said Eli, pulling his nose away from the picture on the wall. "But how do we rescue the umbrella? It's way up on the highest point of the roof."

Eli opened the window.

Boom.

Thunder rumbled up above. The dark gray clouds were a safe distance away, but the storm was still there, drifting lazily across the sky.

Eli stuck his head outside the window and noticed a small ledge, hardly big enough to stand on. Many of the wooden shingles had fallen off. There were plenty of holes in the roof that would be perfect for climbing, but the rain made everything so slippery.

"There's no chance of climbing up the roof," said Eli. "We're on the fourth floor. If I slip and fall..." He gulped. "That's a long drop to the bottom."

Grace wiggled her lips back and forth like she did sometimes when she was thinking hard.

"Magic junk?" she suggested.

"Yeah, good idea," said Eli. "But how? All we have left are these shoelaces. I guess we could tie them all together and make a long rope."

Eli dug into his front jeans pocket and pulled out the handful of used shoelaces that Uncle Larry had given him. Black laces, white laces, brown laces, and about half a dozen other colors.

Zip!

At first, the shoelaces hung loose in Eli's hand. Then something odd happened. The shoelaces twitched, wiggled, then suddenly began to wrap themselves around his wrist. He laughed it off for a moment, right up until the shoelaces started to wrap around his whole body.

"HELP!" cried Eli. "These shoelaces are attacking me! Get them off!"

The magic shoelaces were spinning, looping, and knotting themselves tight around Eli's body.

"Hold still, will you? And stop shouting in my ear," said Grace, trying to help her brother break free. "Why are you yelling? Does it hurt?"

"No, it doesn't hurt!" shouted Eli. "But how would you like it if shoelaces were attacking you?"

It was no use trying to pry off the shoelaces. There were hundreds of them, all intertwined. And the knots were too tight to pull free.

"Help!" cried Eli. "Killer shoelaces!"

Grace's eyes grew wide when she looked down at the floor. "Um, Eli? You have a bigger problem than shoelaces attacking you."

Eli's feet weren't touching the floor!

"Oh no," groaned Eli. "What's wrong with me now? I'm under some kind of magic spell!"

Grace giggled. "There's nothing wrong with you, Eli," she told him. "You're inflatable!"

Eli didn't laugh. "Just get me down!"

Instead of helping her brother get back to his feet, or stand on solid ground, Grace did something else.

Clunk.

She opened the window all the way. Big enough so that a person could fit through.

"What are you doing?" asked Eli, nervously. "Don't you dare send me outside. I'm going to drift away like a weather balloon!"

Grace told him to relax. "No, you're not," she said, pushing him toward the open window. He really was as light as a balloon. "You are going to go up there and get that umbrella."

Eli shouted, "Wait!"

"Sorry, Eli. There's no time!" Grace gave him a hard shove and sent him out the window.

Whoosh!

Just like a kite, Eli flew up into the air! Soon he was ten…twenty…thirty feet from the house, and drifting higher into the night sky.

Grace held tight, until the very last shoelace was in her grasp. A blue one, which was only hanging on by a few threads. But she didn't dare tell her brother that. Eli was scared enough already. A gust of wind came along and turned him the wrong way.

"Grace, help me!" shouted Eli, now upside-down. "Pull me back inside! You can have my rollerblades! And my skateboard! And my bike! Anything! Just pull me in!"

Grace tried her best to reassure him. "Eli, we have to get that umbrella," she hollered. "You are not going to float away, I promise. Do you still have the fan?"

Eli took a few deep breaths, then he searched his pockets. "Yes, I still have it. But what am I supposed to do with a fan while I'm up here?"

The night turned quiet for a moment.

"Oh. Right!" The sparkle in Eli's eyes revealed that he knew exactly what to do.

Click.

The fan turned on, and he was suddenly moving through the air. Slowly at first, but at least he was headed in the right direction—up.

"Good thinking!" shouted Eli, who was now smiling instead of yelling for help. "I just wish you would've told me what you were doing before pushing me out the window!"

"Sorry!" Grace called up to her inflatable brother. "I promise to give you more warning the next time you turn into a hot air balloon!"

Whrrrrrrrr…

With the help of the mini fan, inflatable Eli was pushed right up to the tip-top of the roof. It took a couple of tries, since it was really stuck in there, but he was finally able to pull the umbrella free.

"Got it!" cheered Eli. His happy expression quickly disappeared when something slipped from his fingers. "Oh no!"

Thunk.

They both heard the plastic mini fan thump, bump, and clunk off the roof before it tumbled down to the ground.

"Don't worry!" Grace called up to him. "I've got you! Just hold on tight!"

A moment later, Eli was pulled back into the room, just like winding up the string of a kite.

"That was great!" said Eli, a huge grin on his face. "Scary, but fun." Mostly he was glad that his feet were back on solid ground.

Zip! Zip! Zip!

As soon as Eli was back safe inside the witch's room, the magic shoelaces dropped to the floor in a large pile.

"Nice work up there," said Grace.

"Thanks." Eli gave his sister a hi-five. "You were great too. And we completed everything! We rescued the cat and found Misty's umbrella."

All they had to do now was figure out how to get home. To do that, they would need some help.

It was time to wake up the witch.

16
Storm Chasers

"Do you want to wake her up?" Grace pointed to the doll laying on the bed. "Be careful, though. She doesn't wake up quietly."

Eli felt brave after retrieving the umbrella from the roof, so he agreed to wake up the weather witch.

"Sure, no problem," he said, then reached out his hand to touch the doll.

Poof!

Another bright flash burst in the air, and a great cloud of purple smoke filled the room.

"Are you okay?" asked Eli.

"Yes, I'm fine," said Grace, waving her hands back and forth. "I just can't see anything."

When the smoke finally settled, they quickly realized that something important was missing from the room.

The doll was gone.

"Where'd she go?" said Grace, looking all around. "There's nowhere to hide in this room."

Eli checked under the bed. "Nope, she's not hiding there," he said. "I didn't mean to make her disappear. How are we supposed to get home?"

The room went quiet.

"We can't be stuck here," said Grace. "Can we?"

Eli wasn't sure. But before either of them could get too worried…

"Yoo-hoo! Eli and Grace!" called a familiar voice. "Down here, my dears!"

From the open window came the cheerful sound of the weather witch calling their names. Misty didn't disappear. She was in the front yard, waving up at them.

"Come down!" called Misty. "I have one more surprise I want to show you. You'll love it!"

Eli and Grace ran downstairs, out the front door, and down the porch steps.

The weather witch was dancing in the air.

"Nice work, both of you!" Misty blew them a kiss full of purple sparks. "You did a wonderful job this evening. And fast, too! I've had other kids, some older than you, who took twice as long to rescue Smokey."

Eli held out the witch's umbrella. "Here you go," he said. "This belongs to you."

Misty graciously accepted the gift. "Thank you, Eli. I'll need this to take you back." She opened the umbrella and a gust of wind pulled her up into the air. She cackled with delight, and twirled around until it made them dizzy just to watch.

"I'm glad you brought your scooters with you," said Misty. "Otherwise it would take much longer to get back to Uncle Larry's. And there might be a lot of explaining to do if you two don't show up until the wee morning hours."

Eli and Grace were both wondering how late it was. It felt like they'd been gone a long time.

"Your dad has finished taking apart the fan blades," Misty went on. "We must hurry, but I think we'll make it just in time to avoid a lengthy explanation." She winked.

Eli and Grace were very proud of all their hard work, but agreed that it was time to head back.

Their scooters were right where they'd left them, leaning against the post at the bottom of the front porch steps.

"We have to ride our scooters all the way back to Uncle Larry's?" asked Grace. "That's really far."

Eli's legs felt tired simply at the thought of pushing up that long, steep hill they rode down.

Misty's fingers crackled with purple light. "Don't worry. We're going to take a shortcut."

Zap!

A blast of colorful sparks rained down on their scooters. When the cloud of smoke disappeared, they saw that the handlebars, wheels, and seats had been modified.

"Flying scooters?" said Eli. "Cool!"

The weather witch had magically changed their push scooters into something much faster.

Scooters with *wings*.

"Up, up, up we go!" said the weather witch as she drifted higher into the night sky. "Follow me, my dears! I'll show you the fastest way back to Uncle Larry's. Hold on tight! And don't forget to wear your raincoats!"

Eli gave his sister a funny look. "Raincoats?"

Grace shrugged. "Sure, why not." She reached into her back pocket and pulled out the plastic grocery bag. As soon as she poked a hole in the bag and slipped it on...

Zap!

The plastic bag turned into a yellow rain slicker, just her size.

"Race you up there!" said Grace, then quickly took off on her flying scooter.

"Hey, wait for me!" Eli fumbled a bit, but he was finally able to poke a hole through the stretchy plastic and slip the bag over his head. The plastic bag Uncle Larry had given him magically turned into a raincoat, exactly his size.

Now it was time to chase the storm!

"That's it, my dears," said Misty as they flew single file through the air. "Hurry! We have to make it back before your dad finds you."

Soon they were hundreds of feet in the air. The weather witch kept leading them higher and higher, until the storm was getting close.

Thunder shook the sky.

During the speedy ride, Eli thought back to the severe storm they'd just survived. And now they were chasing after it!

By the time Eli caught up to his sister, she had stopped in mid-air. The town of Weatherville was somewhere down below.

"We have to wait for her signal," explained Grace, keeping a close eye on the witch. "Then we have to fly directly into the storm, exactly where she's pointing. Otherwise…"

Eli gave her a nervous look. "Otherwise what?"

Grace shrugged. "The weather witch wouldn't

tell me," she said. "My guess is that she doesn't really know what would happen."

Hovering in the air high above the storm, they waited for the signal. The rain was really coming down. Their rain jackets helped, but getting wet was the least of their problems.

BOOM.

More thunder.

A flash of lightning ripped across the sky. Clouds of gray and black swirled around in a huge circle—a *cyclone*.

"That's not just a regular storm," said Eli, floating in the air next to his sister. "I think it's a hurricane."

Even in the dark, it was easy to tell that the storm had grown immensely. At the center was a dark circle, where everything appeared calm, even though the storm was raging all around.

"The weather witch wants us to fly right through it," said Grace, shielding herself from the rain. "Look, she's waving at us!"

Not far below, Misty the weather witch was waving her arms and pointing her umbrella toward the center of the cyclone, sometimes called the *eye of the storm*.

"On the count of three!" hollered the weather witch. "One…"

"Two…" said Grace.

"Three!" shouted Eli.

Vrrooooom!

Two flying scooters took off across the sky. Eli and Grace sped toward the exact spot in the storm where Misty was pointing. As they zoomed past the weather witch, they could just make out the words, "Bye, dears! I hope to see you again soon!"

A huge flash of purple light filled the sky.

Eli and Grace raced their scooters as fast as they could. At the last moment, they both closed their eyes, squeezing the handlebars tight.

Zap!

They were gone.

17
Junkyard Olympics

Bloop!

Eli came flying out of the junkyard door first. He sailed head over heels, completely out of control.

"Whoa!" shouted Eli, then landed with a soft thump on the mattresses that Uncle Larry had set up earlier in the day. He bounced from one mattress set to the other, then slammed onto the hard cement floor. His landing needed a lot of work, but he was glad to be back safe inside Uncle Larry's store.

There was just one problem…

He was alone.

"Grace?" Eli hurried over to junkyard door to look for his sister. Outside was nothing but the same old junky cars, rusty garden tools, and rows of used appliances.

"Are you out here?" called Eli. "If you're fooling around, please stop. I need to know you're safe."

For one brief moment, a terrible thought entered his mind. He worried that Grace had made a wrong turn and was now lost inside the storm.

Eli didn't need to worry. The weather witch's shortcut had worked just fine. But he did need to get out of the way in a hurry.

Bloop!

Grace came blasting out of the junkyard door and went sailing twenty feet across the store. She bounced harmlessly off the mattresses, then sprang to her feet like an Olympic athlete.

"Ta-da!" Grace took a bow. "See? All my dance classes are definitely worth it."

Eli applauded. "Nice landing, Grace! I had more of a crash landing. But your dismount was really good. I'm impressed."

Dad, unfortunately, was *not* impressed.

"Oh. Hey, Dad." Eli waved.

"Hi, Dad!" Grace smiled innocently.

Dad had a strange look on his face. He was trying to understand what he'd just seen. It appeared as if his daughter had just come shooting out of the junkyard door like a rocket, bounced a few times, then landed perfectly on her feet.

"I hope you two aren't causing any trouble back here," said Dad with a look of warning. "I don't think Uncle Larry would be too pleased if he found out that you were using these mattresses for a trampoline."

Eli and Grace couldn't stop laughing. Flying through the storm was amazing! But they had to keep a straight face or risk getting in trouble.

"We weren't, Dad," said Eli. "I promise."

Grace nodded that it was true. "Did you and Uncle Larry get the paddles down?" she asked, quickly changing the subject.

Their dad was holding two long kayak paddles in his arms, so Uncle Larry's paddle fan must now be ruined.

"Hm? Oh! Yes, we did," said Dad, then held up the paddles to show them. "It took longer than expected, but Uncle Larry helped." He paused, then added, "Well, I did most of the work, while Uncle Larry held the ladder."

When they went to the checkout counter, they found Uncle Larry in his usual spot, sitting on his favorite brown leather stool. Leaning back, he was trying to feel the cool air blowing down from the one lonely blade left on the ceiling fan.

Wuzz, wuzz, wuzz.

"Sorry, Ben," said Uncle Larry. "It's just not the same anymore. But I'm sure glad you and the kids will have fun with the inflatable kayak thingy. I guess I'll just have to find something else to use for my ceiling fan blades. Maybe there's some more cardboard around here that I can use…"

Eli and Grace stood on the other side of the counter. They both had the biggest smiles on their faces after getting back from one of the wildest junkyard adventures they'd had so far.

"Hi, Uncle Larry!" said Grace.

Uncle Larry sat up so fast that he fell off the stool with a muffled *crash*. The pile of vintage throw pillows he was saving for another customer broke his fall.

"Eli! Grace!" said Uncle Larry, getting to his feet. "You're back!" His bushy eyebrows raised to the middle of his forehead when he realized he almost gave away the secret. "I mean, you're back from the, um…"

"Back of the store!" suggested Grace.

Uncle Larry winked and gave them a quick thumbs-up as he smoothed out his thinning hair.

Dad gave them all a funny look. Before he could ask any more questions, Uncle Larry rang up their purchase.

"Let's see, two paddles at one dollar each…" Uncle Larry brought out his clunky old calculator with the $9.00 price tag. "That'll be two dollars."

Their dad handed the store owner a couple of dollar bills. Then he watched curiously as Uncle Larry scribbled the sale down on a sticky note, even though he'd installed a new bookkeeping program for him a few weeks ago—of course, that was after they'd found his computer, which was buried under years' worth of papers, clutter, and junk.

"Don't worry, Ben," said Uncle Larry. "I'll enter the sale into that bookkeeping…app thingy…just as soon as I close up the store."

Dad laughed. "I'm glad the new bookkeeping system is working, Larry."

Uncle Larry had a tough time trying to fit such a long, awkward purchase into a regular sized bag. He ended up slapping a sticky note on the end of each paddle: SOLD.

18
Peeking Through the Clouds

Dad lifted the tailgate of the SUV and jumped back in surprise. The inflatable kayak was right where it should be. But it wasn't deflated like it was when they'd arrived at Uncle Larry's.

The kayak was fully blown up! It took up so much room that there was no way they could drive home with it like that.

"Did you two do this?" asked Dad. "You both know the rules. You're not allowed to leave the store by yourselves."

The foot pump was right there, so it was perfectly reasonable to think they'd left Uncle Larry's store and gone out to the car.

"Well, you see, Dad…" Eli wasn't going to lie, but telling the truth about how they'd needed the kayak for a cat rescue probably wouldn't go over well. It would sound like they were making up a story so they wouldn't get in trouble. There was no way their dad would believe they'd inflated the kayak while inside their junkyard adventure.

"We both did it," admitted Grace. "Sorry, Dad. We were just so excited to have the kayak that we, um…wanted to test it out."

Dad didn't get mad. He was just glad the used inflatable kayak didn't seem to have any holes.

"Next time, just tell me if you're going to leave the store," said Dad. "Do we have a deal?"

"Deal," they said.

When the kayak was deflated, everyone piled into the car and out of the rain. Dad started the car and everyone got buckled up, ready for home.

"I just have one question," said Dad. He

adjusted the rear view mirror so he could see them properly in the back seat.

"Yes, Dad?"

With a grin, he asked, "Why are you both wearing a plastic grocery bag?"

Grace laughed. "We were just playing a game," she said as she pulled off her magic raincoat.

"Yeah," said Eli. "A witchy weather game."

While stuck in the line of traffic waiting to turn left onto Broadway Street, the whole car was suddenly filled with sunlight.

"Hey, look!" Dad pointed out the window. "It finally stopped raining."

The sun was peeking through the clouds.

"Perfect timing too," said Dad. The *squeak-squeak-squeak* of the windshield wipers was so loud that Grace had to cover her ears.

"Are they broken?" she asked.

"Yes, honey," said Dad. "Well, not exactly broken. The windshield wipers need to be replaced. And come to think of it…"

"What, Dad?"

Dad had a thoughtful look on his face. "When I was searching for the tools to take down the paddle fan, I'm pretty sure I saw a section of Uncle Larry's store that had all sorts of discounted cars parts, including windshield wipers."

Eli wiggled his eyebrows at his sister. Grace was thinking the same thing. Soon it would be time for another junkyard adventure.

"Ready for home?" asked Dad when it was their turn to pull out onto Broadway.

"Ready," said Eli and Grace.

As they headed home in the late afternoon traffic, Dad turned on some music. There was no need to listen to the weather report anymore. The dark clouds were leaving, and the sun was shining. The storm was gone—like magic.

"Who knows," said Dad as they drove down the road. "Maybe next time I'm back this way, I'll stop by and see if Larry has the right size windshield wipers to fit our vehicle."

Eli and Grace exchanged an excited look. From the back seat, they asked, "Can we go too?"

Thank you for reading Book 8 of the **Junkyard Adventures** series. I hope you enjoyed visiting Uncle Larry's Antique Shop & Junkyard.

If you have time to leave a review, I would appreciate it! If you would like to go on more adventures with Eli and Grace, please check out the other books in the **JYA** series.

Let's experiment with WEATHER!

The weather witch knows a lot about all sorts of weather—especially storms. Here is one kind of storm you can try creating at home. It's called…

Snowstorm

Here is a list of the **main** things you will need:

1) Water

2) Glass Jar

3) Baby Oil

4) White Paint

5) Alka Seltzer

And here are a few other things that will help to make this weather project a little bit easier…and a little less messy.

Bowl (to mix the paint).

Glitter (for added stormy effect).

Paper towels (for cleaning up any spills).

Ready for some wild weather? Follow the steps on the next two pages to make your own snowstorm in a jar!

Step 1

Gather all your supplies and find a place to work on your weather experiment.

Step 2

Add the baby oil to your jar. You can add up to 3/4 full, but leave enough room for the colored paint.

Step 3

Mix the paint and water in a separate bowl. White paint works well, but you can use any color you like.

Step 4

Pour in the white paint, adding it to the baby oil.

Step 5

Add a little glitter for some extra stormy weather. (Optional).

Then add the Alka-Seltzer tablets one at a time.

Repeat these steps as many times as you like!

Your snowstorm should be swirling around inside the jar!
When the first storm is over, add another tablet and watch it
fizz and bubble all over again.

Now try creating a storm with a different color of paint. Or
for a really wild storm, you could add 2 tablets and make a
"blizzard" in a jar.

Let's make some MORE weather!

This next one is called…

Raincloud

Here is a list of the **main** things you will need:

1) Glass Jar

2) Water Colors

3) Shaving Cream

4) Glitter

5) Pipette (eyedropper)

Step 1

Fill the jar 2/3 of the way full of water.

Step 2

Add LOTS of shaving cream. The "cloud" can even go high above the rim of the glass jar.

Step 3

In a separate bowl, mix the water color. Blue works well, but any color will do. The **darker** the color, the better the experiment will work.

Step 4

Time to add color! Use the eyedropper (pipette) to drip the water color down through the shaving cream. Add color slowly and watch the "raincloud" appear.

Repeat these steps as many times as you like!

This next one is called...

Soap Tornado

Here is a list of the **main** things you will need:

1) Glass Jar

2) Water

3) Dish Soap

4) Glitter

Step 1

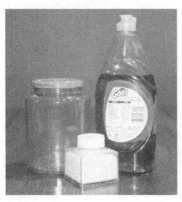

Gather all your supplies and find a place to work on this next swirling, twirling, high-speed weather experiment.

Step 2

Fill the glass jar with water, then add the glitter. You can add a little glitter, or a lot. (Try both and see what happens!)

Step 3

Add a small amount of soap. This time you don't want to add too much, or else the weather experiment might get too bubbly.

Step 4

Now swirl the jar around as fast as you can, then watch the "tornado" spin. (Make sure to put the lid on first!)

Repeat these steps as many times as you like!

What constellation will you find with the Alien of Astronomy?

A JUNKYARD ADVENTURE

Alien of Astronomy

TEVIN HANSEN

A JUNKYARD ADVENTURE

Mermaid of Music

Music Crafts Inside

TEVIN HANSEN

Make a beautiful melody with the Mermaid of Music.

A JUNKYARD ADVENTURE

Art Monster

CRAFT PROJECTS INSIDE

TEVIN HANSEN

Get creative with the Art Monster.

Follow the Author

Sign up for my **newsletter** to receive
all the latest book news at:

www.TevinHansen.com

Made in United States
North Haven, CT
18 September 2022

24290659R00082